SIMON & SCHUSTER BOOKS FOR YOUNG READERS
An imprint of Simon & Schuster Children's Publishing Division
1230 Avenue of the Americas, New York, New York 10020
Text copyright © 2001 by Tony Bonning
Illustrations copyright © 2001 by Sally Hobson
First published as STONE SOUP in Great Britain in 2001 by Gullane Children's Books,
a division of Gullane Entertainment Plc.
First U.S. edition 2002
All rights reserved, including the right of reproduction in whole or in part in any form.
SIMON & SCHUSTER BOOKS FOR YOUNG READERS is a trademark of Simon & Schuster.
The text for this book is set in 20-point Tempus Sans.
Printed in Hong Kong
2 4 6 8 10 9 7 5 3 1
CIP data for this book is available from the Library of Congress.
ISBN 0-689-84900-1

Fox Tale Soup

Tony Bonning

Illustrated by Sally Hobson

Simon & Schuster Books for Young Readers
New York   London   Toronto   Sydney   Singapore

One afternoon, a tired and hungry fox stopped at a farm gate.

"Can you spare a little food for a hungry traveler?" he asked.

"No!" said Cow.
"I don't have any extra," said Donkey.
"Not me," said Goat.
"No! No! No! No!" said the four hens.
"Go away!" said Old Dog.

"Well, may I trouble you for a drop of water to make some soup?" asked Fox.

Sheep, who was slightly
kinder than the others,
brought some water
in a bucket.

Fox lit a fire, took a pot
from his backpack,
poured in the water,
and put it on the fire.

Soon the water was bubbling away.

Fox carefully chose a stone, sniffed it, and dropped it into the water. "That should make a fine pot of stone soup," he said.

Full of curiosity, the animals gathered closer as Fox took a spoon from his bag, dipped it in the water, and had a taste. "Mmm! Delicious!" he said. "But it's not quite right."

"I think it needs a touch of salt and pepper. Do you have any?" he asked Sheep.

Sheep fetched some salt and pepper and Fox put it in the pot.
The puzzled animals moved closer as Fox took a sip.

But still the soup wasn't quite right.

Fox thought perhaps
a taste of turnip might do it.
Cow went to her shed, chose
a turnip and gave it to Fox, who
chopped it up and put it in the pot.
Fox took a long sniff and a small sip . . .

But still the soup wasn't quite right.

Fox wondered
if a hint of
carrot would do
the trick.
Donkey knew just
where to find one and
so trotted off to get it.

He came back with a large carrot, which also
was chopped up and dropped into the pot . . .

But still the soup wasn't quite right.

Fox thought something was missing. . . .
Of course! It needed a cabbage!
Goat hot-trotted off to get one.
By now the animals were leaning right over
the steaming pot, their mouths watering . . .

But *still* the soup wasn't quite right.

Fox was sure a sprinkling of corn
would be the finishing touch.
The hens dashed away and rushed back with
bowls of corn, which also were tipped into the pot.

The soup bubbled and boiled,
and the animals licked their lips.

At last, the stone soup
was just right. They all
shared it . . . down to
the very last, delicious
drop.

Everyone agreed it was the best soup they'd
ever tasted. Even Old Dog said so. "And all
from a stone!" he said.
"Amazing," they all agreed.

"Well, time to go," said
Fox, putting on his backpack.
All the animals wished him luck and
told him to stop and make another pot
of stone soup, if he ever passed the farm again.
"Thank you," said Fox, with a wily smile. "I certainly will."

And he set off,
down the road.